The Monkey Bridge

by Rafe Martin

illustrated by Fahimeh Amiri

Alfred A. Knopf
New York

For Philip Kapleau, Roshi, and all bridge-builders
—R. M.

To my family and dear friend Ralph, with love
—F. A.

THIS IS A BORZOI BOOK PUBLISHED BY ALFRED A. KNOPF, INC.

Text copyright © 1997 by Rafe Martin
Illustrations copyright © 1997 by Fahimeh Amiri
All rights reserved under International and Pan-American Copyright Conventions. Published in the United States of America
by Alfred A. Knopf, Inc., New York, and simultaneously in Canada by Random House of Canada Limited, Toronto.
Distributed by Random House, Inc., New York.
http://www.randomhouse.com/

Printed in Singapore
10 9 8 7 6 5 4 3 2 1

Library of Congress Cataloging-in-Publication Data

Martin, Rafe.
The monkey bridge / written by Rafe Martin ; illustrated by Fahimeh Amiri.
p.   cm.
Summary: A human king learns wisdom and compassion from a monkey king
willing to make a great sacrifice for the good of his subjects.
ISBN 0-679-88106-9 (trade) — ISBN 0-679-98106-3 (lib. bdg.)
1. Jataka stories, English.   [1. Jataka stories.]   I. Title.
BQ1462.E5M37   1997
294.3'823—dc20   96-27974

Author's Note

The Monkey Bridge is a retelling of a traditional Buddhist jataka tale. Over five hundred such stories exist, each recounting a different past lifetime of the Buddha when, as an animal or human, god or spirit, he exerted himself to inspire greater wisdom and compassion. These stories are an expression of the mythic thinking of Buddhism. To believers they suggest that when the Buddha was born in India as the historical prince Siddhartha Gautama 2,500 years ago, he had already prepared well for his Enlightenment. After Enlightenment, Prince Siddhartha was known as the Buddha, meaning simply "the Awakened One."

These tales have come down to us in two primary collections: *The Jataka*— a lengthy anthology of jataka tales and poems in the ancient Pali language of Southeast Asia, and *The Jatakamala* of the Sanskrit poet Aryasura. ("Jatakamala" means a garland or rosary of jatakas. This is a neat little verbal reminder of the Buddha's own teachings, which are called sutras—meaning words "strung together as beads on a thread.") The story of *The Monkey Bridge* is one of the most famous jatakas and appears in both texts. (Other texts once existed, but they have been lost.) This version has been inspired by Aryasura's.

For 2,500 years, jataka tales have remained one of the most popular of all kinds of stories.

I especially like *The Monkey Bridge* because it shows a human being learning wisdom from an animal. And I like it too, because it emphasizes compassion, the most noble of virtues.

In the heart
of Benares,
one of the oldest cities
in the world, grows a tree.
So delicious is its fruit
that people say the tree grew
from a seed that fell from heaven.
Storytellers, however, know more of the tale.
And they tell this story about it.

Long ago a tree grew high in the Himalaya Mountains, the highest mountains on this earth. The fruit of the tree was fragrant as perfume and more delicious than any food imaginable. A tribe of monkeys lived in the tree, clambering from branch to branch, racing along the mighty limbs, swinging by their tails, eating the sweet fruit, and sleeping peacefully at night curled among the green leaves.

They called their wonderful tree-home "the Treasure Tree."

At that time a great monkey king kept peace among all the monkeys, settling their disputes and guarding them from danger.

One day the Monkey King realized: any fruit that fell from the Treasure Tree into the river would be carried swiftly downstream. "Then in some village or town or city far down the mountainside," he said, "the fruit will be found. Because of its fragrant odor and heavenly taste, people will prize it. They will search for our tree to find the source of the fruit. Then we will be in danger."

So every evening, as the sun began to set, the Monkey King would say, "Remember, my dear subjects, any fruit that ripens over the water must be plucked lest it fall into the river and be washed away."

And the monkeys would always answer, "It is being done at this very moment, Great King." And the Monkey King would be content.

But one evening a tiny fruit was overlooked. Leaves hung thickly all around it. Unnoticed, day by day the fruit grew larger and riper. Then one night it dropped with a little splash into the river. Bobbing on the starlit, foaming water, it was carried off by the current and was soon out of sight.

The next morning, far down the mountain, in the ancient city of Benares, a king sat upon his royal throne. Long lines of petitioners stood before him, each asking for his judgment. "Hear my cause, Worthy King!" called one. "Mercy, Just Ruler!" cried another. "Help me, Sire!" pleaded a third.

His ministers, too, gathered around the throne. "We have a boundary dispute to settle, Sovereign Liege," said one, presenting a series of charts. "There are rumors of war far to the south, Lord," said a second, unrolling a map. "Here are the samples of our recent harvest, Great King," said a third, placing baskets of fruit and grain before the throne.

"No more!" exclaimed the king. "That is all for today. I must relax from my labors. Bring the royal boat. I will set out for a journey in the fresh air on the river."

The king and his attendants arrived at the riverside and went aboard the royal boat. "Take me upstream," he ordered. So the oarsmen rowed against the backbreaking current. "Ah, this is the life," said the king as he leaned on his pillow. Breathing deeply, he watched the sunlight sparkle on the swirling water and the green leaves glisten. "To be king is often burdensome," he said. "My people should take good care of me. Little do they know the stresses of my high office."

The men rowed. The boat forged against the current. After a time the king became aware of a delicious aroma. "What is *that?*" he wondered. "Whatever it is, it must be found! Row, men!" he shouted. "Row there! No, there!" The men rowed from one side of the river to the other.

Suddenly the king cried, "Wait! Something is floating on the water!
Get it for me!" His men rowed forward. A net was flung out, then dragged
back on board. When it was opened, there lay a beautiful fruit—the fruit
of the Treasure Tree!

"It smells delicious!" exclaimed the king. He picked it up and bit into it. "Amazing!" he cried with delight. "It's wonderful! I must have more, much more. Row, men. Row me upstream until we find *my* tree." Once again the oarsmen dutifully bent their backs to it. They rowed and rowed. "Faster!" shouted the king. And his tired men rowed faster.

In time the great Treasure Tree could be seen, spreading its leaves against the sky.

Monkeys raced through the branches, swinging and leaping and eating the delicious fruit.

"What?" roared the king. "Should I, a king among men, let wild creatures eat *my* precious fruit? Archers, draw your bows!"

His bowmen picked up their weapons. The bowstrings were drawn tight and the arrows aimed.

When the monkeys saw the boat approaching, they raced to the
top of the great tree and huddled together, chattering in fear. The
treetop swayed slowly back and forth beneath them.

The Monkey King saw the arrows and at once knew the danger.
"Alas," he said, "the day I feared has come. Humans have found our tree.
I must save my people."

In one great leap he flew from the treetop to the mountain and grasped a sturdy stalk of bamboo growing there. Then he wrapped his long tail around its tip and made another mighty leap back, catching hold of the very end of a branch of the Treasure Tree. No other monkey in the world could have made such a jump. "Run over my back, friends, and escape," called the Monkey King. "Hurry. I will try to hold on until you are safe. Run!"

The terrified monkeys jumped from the branches of the tree and raced, leaping and bounding, over their king. Like a river, they flowed across the bridge made of the Monkey King's body. Finally, the last of them was across and safe. But now their king was so sore and weak he could barely hold on. His fingers and toes loosened and he started to slip.

The King of Benares had been watching in amazement. "Put down your bows!" he ordered. "We must save that noble monkey. Quick, men, bring the net and stretch it beneath him."

The net was brought and held tightly below. "Trust us!" called the king. "Fall and we shall save you."

The Monkey King's strength was gone. At that very moment he fell from the Treasure Tree. The net, the river, the king and his men, the hard, hard ground rushed up to meet him. But the net caught him and broke his fall. Though bruised and exhausted, he was alive and well.

"Have no fear," said the King of Benares. "No one shall harm you. Let there be peace between us.

"Bring soothing ointments and bandages," he now called. Then, with his own hands, this king of men gently rubbed healing balm into the Monkey King's bruises and wounds and wrapped them in soft bandages.

At last, when the Monkey King was resting comfortably, the human king asked, "Why did you risk yourself to save others?"

"I am their king, Your Majesty. It is my job to protect them."

"But if you are king, you are the most important one," responded the human king. "You could have easily escaped. They should be serving and helping you, not you them."

"Perhaps," said the Monkey King quietly, "but if I save myself first, what would happen to my tribe, my family and friends? It is my love for them and my desire to help and protect them that makes me king, not my size or strength."

The human king sat still. He thought and thought. All the while the sun shone down, the river flowed on, and the great tree swayed overhead, its green leaves rustling in the breeze.

"You are right," he said at last. "This is truly what it means to be king. Now I shall repay you for teaching me. I promise that no one shall ever come here to bother you or your people again. I will forget the taste of this sweet fruit. And I shall order all those who attend me to remain silent about your tree."

"Open your hand," said the Monkey King. The King of Benares did so. Then the Monkey King placed in his palm one bright fruit of the tree. "In this fruit is a seed," said the Monkey King. "Take the fruit and plant the seed in your own kingdom. Care for the seedling. Water it well. In time a tree will grow. Share its fruit with your people. From its fruit will come more seeds. Soon there will be enough for all."

The King of Benares was filled with gratitude. "What a splendid gift!" he exclaimed. "The tree will stand in my most beautiful garden. I will share its fruit with all my people. I will never forget our meeting. Go in peace, Great King."

The Monkey King rose to his feet and shook himself. Then, strength renewed, he bounded up to rejoin his people.

The King of Benares and all his attendants sailed back down the river.

The seed was planted. The tree grew and grew. Its sweet fruit ripens to this day.

So the story goes.